ANIMAL SHOWDOWNS

GORILLA VS. LEOPARD

by Teresa Klepinger

Kaleidoscope
Minneapolis, MN

BIGFOOT BOOKS

The Quest for Discovery Never Ends

This edition first published in 2023 by Kaleidoscope Publishing, Inc.

For information regarding permission, write to
Kaleidoscope Publishing, Inc.
6012 Blue Circle Drive
Minnetonka, MN 55343

Library of Congress Control Number
2022937705

ISBN
978-1-64519-572-6 (library bound)
978-1-64519-642-6 (ebook)

Printed in the United States of America.

Precious McKenzie, Developmental Editor

Bigfoot lurks within one of the images in this book. It's up to you to find him!

TABLE OF CONTENTS

Chapter 1

Sneaky vs. Size

Hello, animal lovers! Welcome to the **ULTIMATE SHOWDOWN** series. Today, we will watch the battle of a gorilla versus a leopard. Who will win? The sneakier one? The bigger animal? The one with the best bite? What will the fight be like?

As the battle of the beasts rages, we'll measure them against each other. We'll keep track of the points they score. Whoever has the most points at the end wins!

Gorilla
Species: Gorilla gorilla

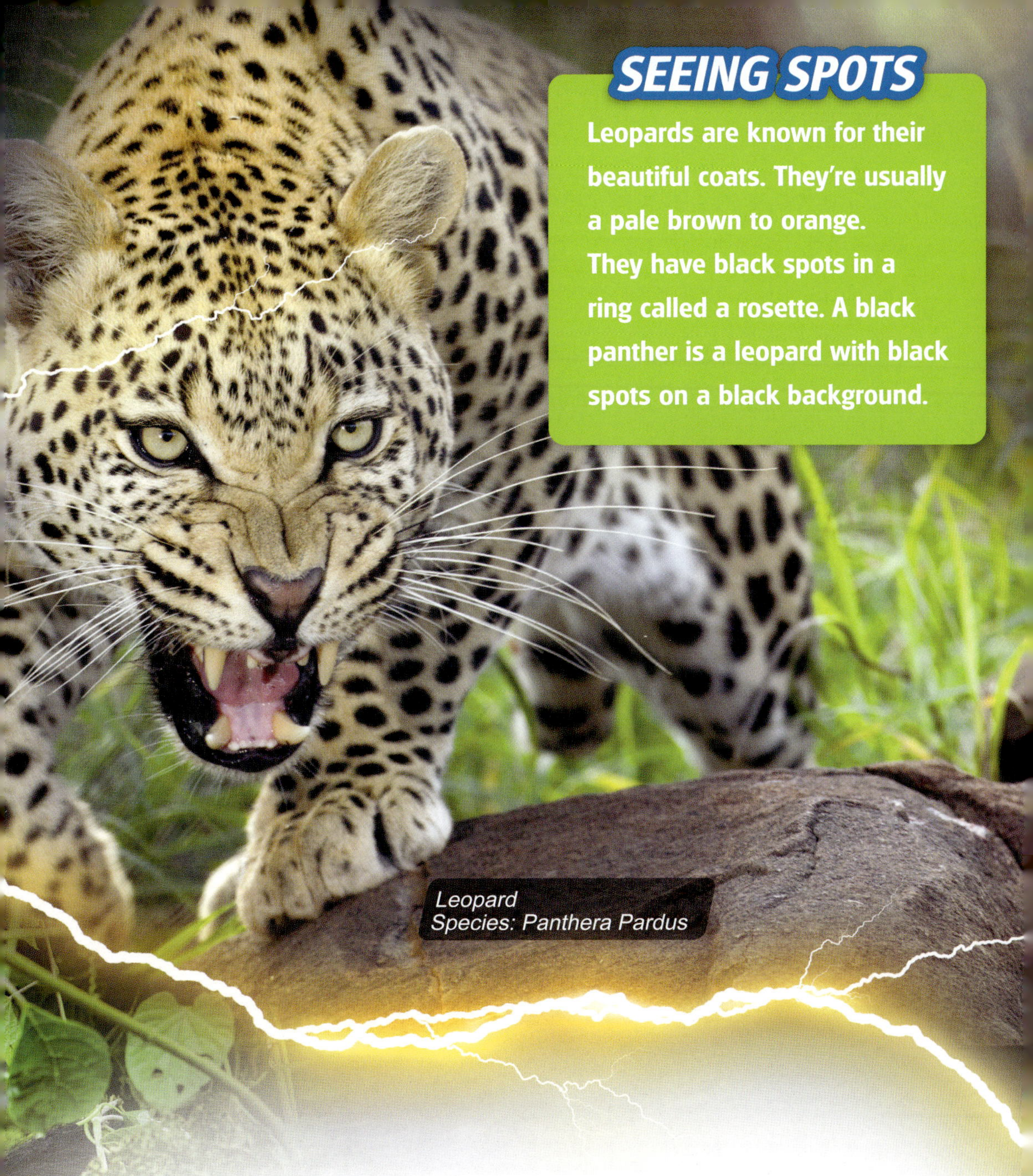

Leopard
Species: Panthera Pardus

SEEING SPOTS

Leopards are known for their beautiful coats. They're usually a pale brown to orange. They have black spots in a ring called a rosette. A black panther is a leopard with black spots on a black background.

The gorilla has no idea the leopard is ready to **ambush** him. The leopard's spotted coat is perfect **camouflage**. He's patient, waiting for just the right moment.

The leopard gathers his legs under him and springs forward. In two jumps, he is on the gorilla's back. All 150 pounds (68 kilograms) of him slams into his **prey**.

If the leopard crashed into an **antelope**, his favorite food, he would easily knock it over. But the gorilla weighs almost 400 pounds (181 kg). He didn't fall over. The leopard bites the gorilla's shoulder. The gorilla is surprised, but he reacts quickly. He grabs the leopard with his hands and pulls him off. That is something an antelope could never do.

The gorilla jumps up onto all fours. He faces the leopard. The leopard crouches low to the ground. He considers what to do next.

FUN FACT

Gorillas have opposable thumbs and big toes. They can touch their other fingers or toes to grab hold of things.

Size Comparison

GORILLA
Height: 5.5 feet (1.7 meters)
Weight: 400 pounds (181 kilograms)

LEOPARD
Length without tail: 6.25 feet (1.9 m)
Length of tail: 4.5 feet (1.4 m)
Weight: 200 pounds (91 kg)

SCOREBOARD

	ROUND 1 SCORE	TOTAL SCORE
Gorilla	8	8
Leopard	10	10

Gorilla

Leopard

crest
long arms

canine teeth

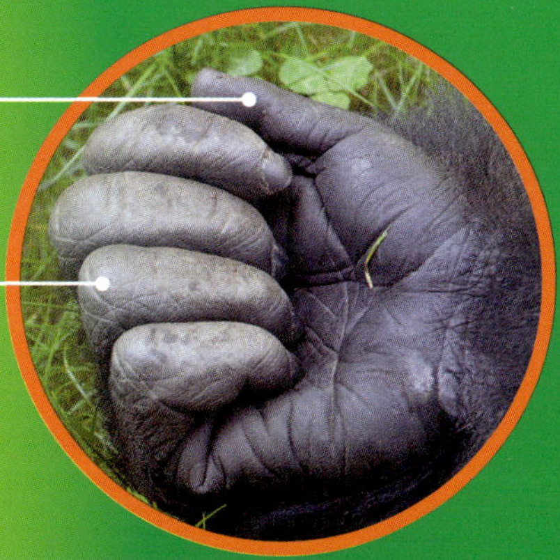
opposable thumbs
knuckles

shoulders
whiskers
claws

canine teeth

Chapter 2

Big and Scary

The gorilla stands up on his legs. Now he is about 5.5 feet (1.68 m) tall. He cups his hands and beats his chest. The loud thumping noises can be heard a half mile (.8 kilometers) away. He roars at the leopard. The gorilla wants to **intimidate** him.

This gorilla is a silverback. When gorillas reach about 12 years old, the hair on their backs turns silver. So this gorilla is grown up and experienced. He has probably had a few fights in his life.

FUN FACT
Young male gorillas are called *blackbacks*. Other gorillas consider them the youngsters of the family.

The leopard stays low. His ears lay back. He hisses and snarls. But he doesn't run off.

SCOREBOARD

	ROUND 2 SCORE	TOTAL SCORE
Gorilla	10	18
Leopard	8	18

The gorilla tries again to scare the leopard away. He lowers himself back onto the knuckles of his third and fourth fingers. Then he runs sideways and tears at the bushes and trees. He pounds the ground. He leans his head back and bares his long **canine teeth**. He even lets out a strong odor from his armpits.

The leopard watches carefully. He's deciding if the gorilla is actually going to attack him.

WHO'S THE SCARIEST?

Gorillas and leopards show certain behaviors to scare away their enemies.

GORILLA: Beating chest, loud noises, tearing up the plants

LEOPARD: Surprise ambush, snarling and spitting, showing fangs

The gorilla screams. Special air pockets in his lungs make the noise even louder. He charges at the leopard. But he still only means to scare the leopard away.

SCOREBOARD

	ROUND 3 SCORE	TOTAL SCORE
Gorilla	10	28
Leopard	7	25

BIG BELLIES!

Gorillas have bellies that are bigger around than their chests. They aren't fat! It's to make room for their extra-long intestines. The extra length is needed to digest all the plants they eat.

Intimidation like this is usually all that's needed to keep gorillas from fighting. They are normally peaceful animals. As **herbivores**, they eat plants and fruit. The closest they come to hunting is digging up termite mounds and ant hills to eat the insects.

Leopards are **carnivores**. They hunt for their food. They eat animals like antelope, wild hogs, monkeys, and rodents. Attacking comes naturally to them.

Where Do GORILLAS AND LEOPARDS Live?

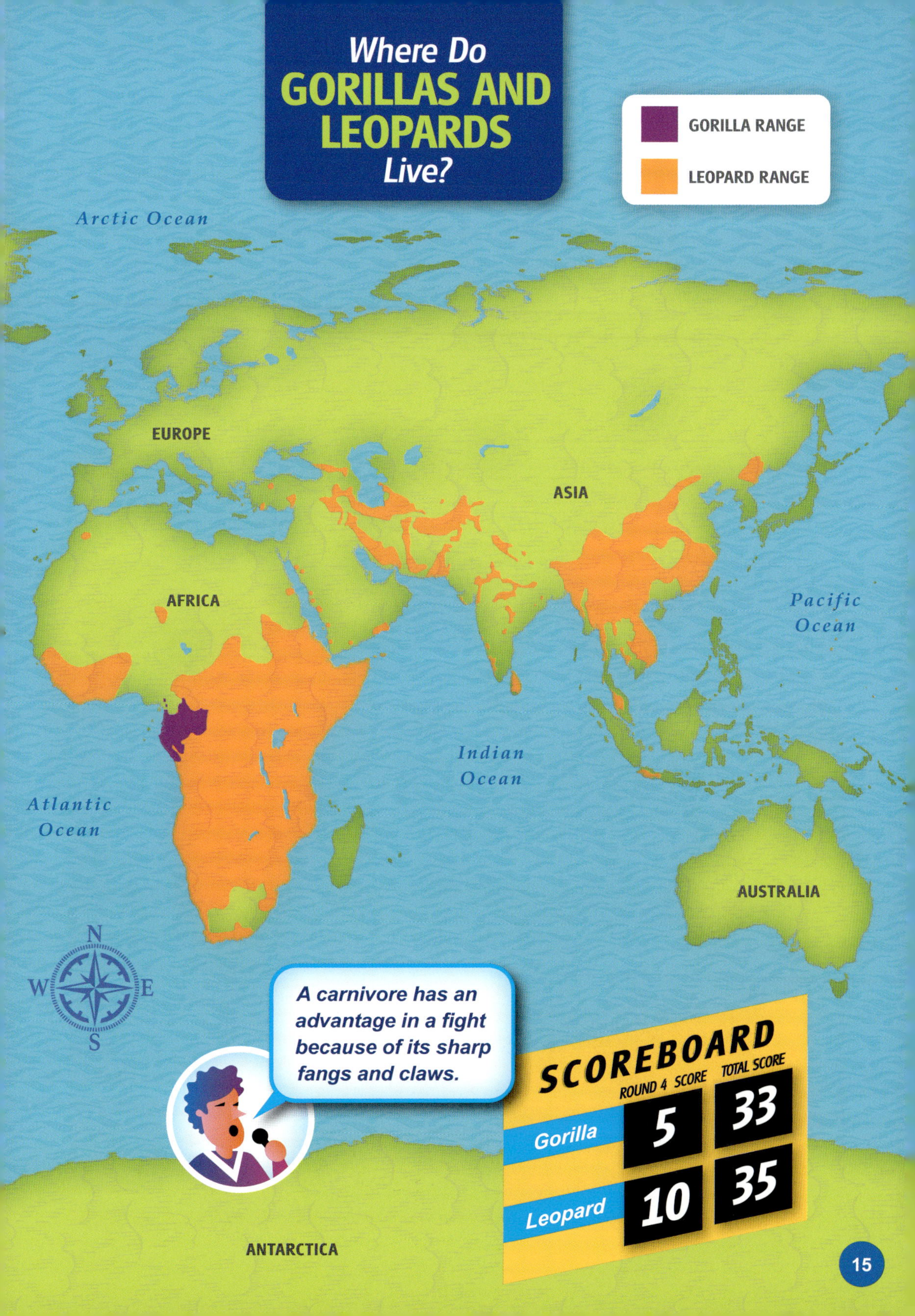

Chapter 3

Making a Move

When the gorilla charges at the leopard, the leopard decides to get out of the way. He jumps up into a tree nearby. Now he's looking down on the gorilla. This is even better for the leopard.

Leopards are excellent tree climbers. They often rest on a branch with their legs dangling on either side. Sometimes they drop headfirst from a tree straight down onto their prey.

FUN FACT

Gorillas have fingerprints like people. No two are alike. They can also be identified by their nose prints!

HEAR THEM ROAR!

Leopards are called big cats, but not just because of their size. Big cats are lions, tigers, cheetahs, and leopards. Big cats are the only cats that can roar. The leopard is the smallest of the big cats.

The leopard wants to be no more than 16 feet (4.8 m) away from the gorilla before he makes his move. The closer he is, the better his chances at success.

Here comes the gorilla again.

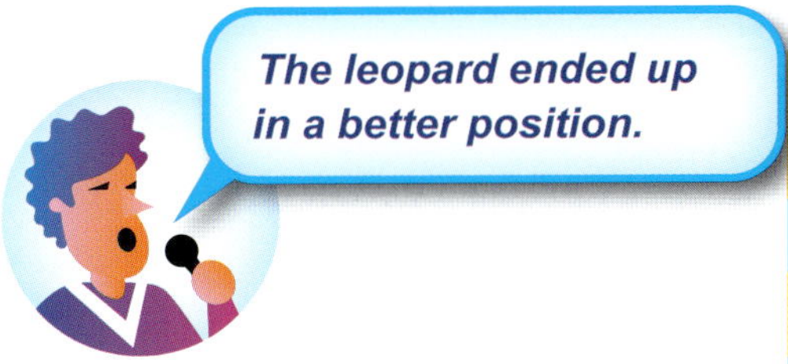

SCOREBOARD

	ROUND 5 SCORE	TOTAL SCORE
Gorilla	6	39
Leopard	10	45

The gorilla picks up a branch he's broken off a tree. As he runs toward the leopard, he swings the branch and roars.

It's just what the leopard was waiting for.

Leopards can jump almost 20 feet (6 m) forward and 10 feet (3 m) straight up. Landing on the gorilla will be easy once he gets close enough.

The gorilla is in the perfect position. The leopard leaps. The big cat and the great ape roll on the ground. Both struggle to get the best position. Gorillas may be peaceful, but they will certainly fight when needed. This gorilla is in a fight for his life.

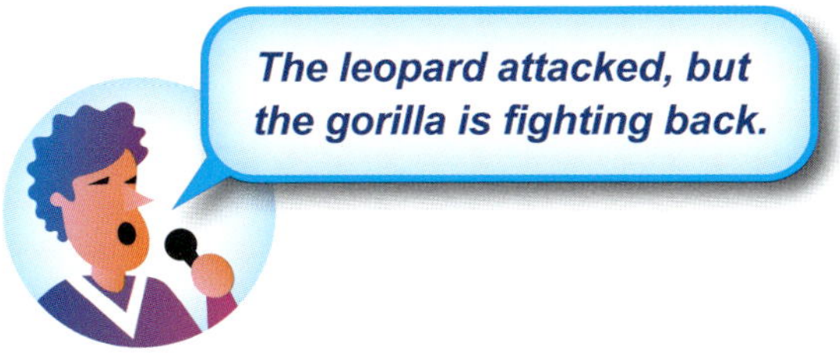

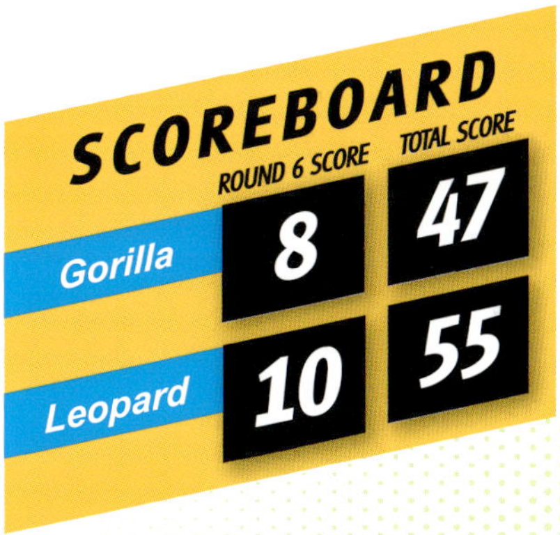

The leopard and the gorilla try to bite each other.

They both have long canine teeth. The leopard's can be almost 1.5 inches (3.8 cm) long. They're perfect for cutting and tearing meat.

Male gorillas have extra-long canine teeth. They use them to defend themselves and to intimidate other males.

The gorilla tries to bite the leopard any way he can. Many bites can cause a lot of blood loss. This would weaken the leopard.

The leopard knows how to kill his prey with one strong bite to the neck. This either chokes it or cuts its spinal cord. He tries to find the right spot on the gorilla.

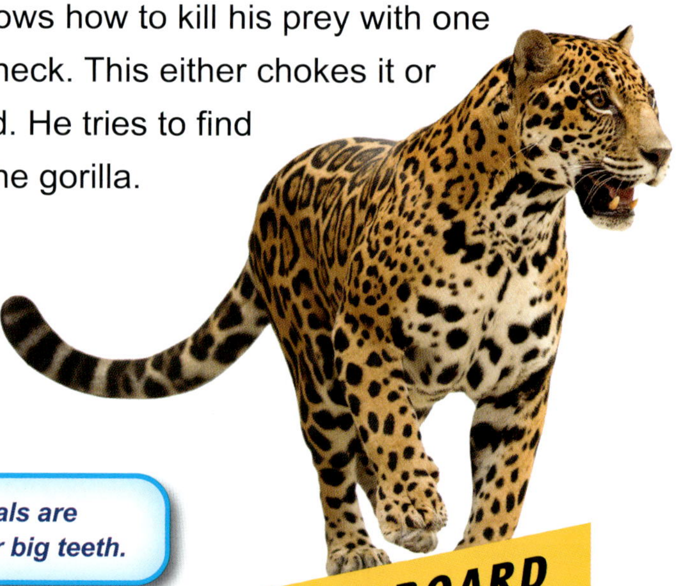

SCOREBOARD

	ROUND 7 SCORE	TOTAL SCORE
Gorilla	10	57
Leopard	10	65

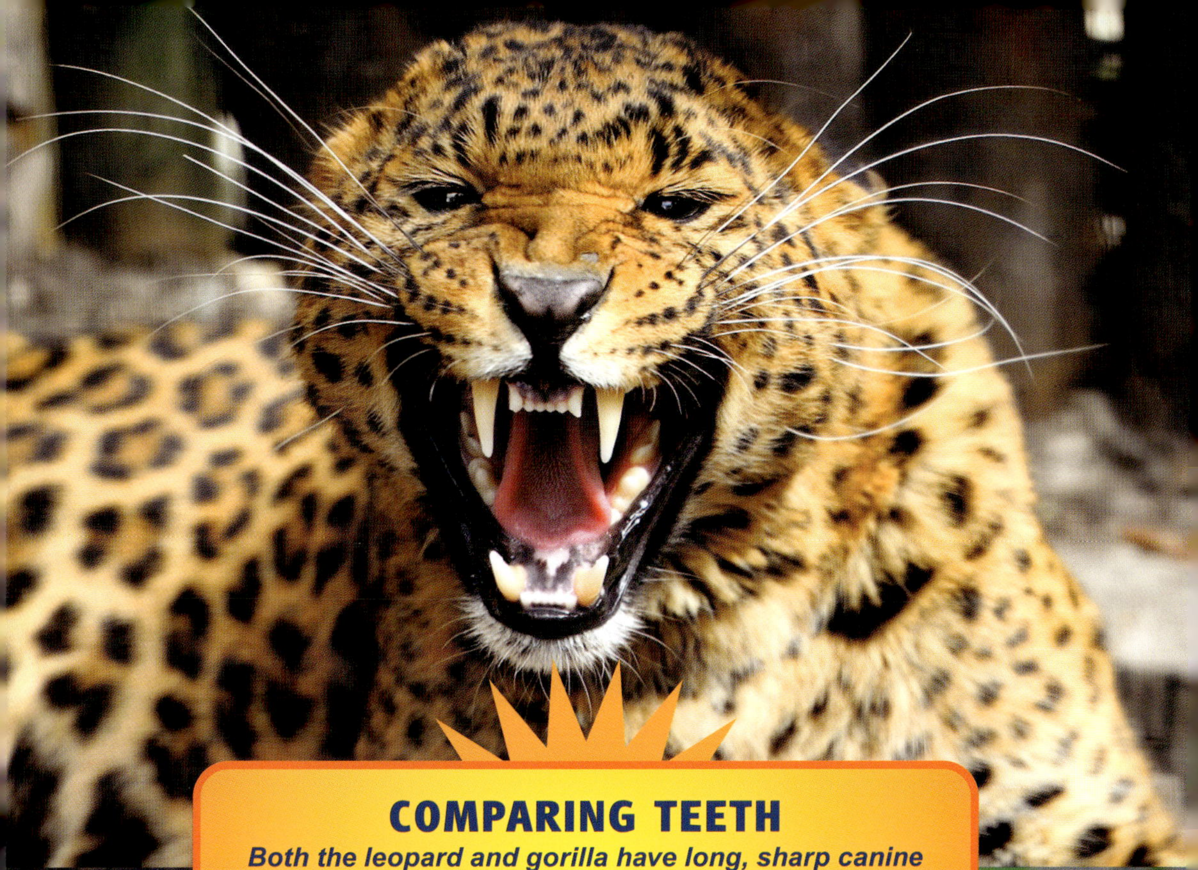

COMPARING TEETH

Both the leopard and gorilla have long, sharp canine teeth. Leopards use their teeth to kill prey. Gorillas use their teeth to scare off enemies or defend themselves.

Chapter 4

Weapons or Luck?

The leopard sinks his teeth into the gorilla's neck. The gorilla's neck is much thicker than an antelope's neck. This time, the leopard's bite doesn't break the gorilla's spine.

The gorilla reaches for the leopard's leg. Gorillas have long arms, even longer than their legs. This helps them walk on all fours. Their arms and shoulders together are also very strong. Some scientists believe gorillas are six times stronger than humans.

BEST WEAPONS

***GORILLA:* Long arms, hands to grab hold, upper body strength, long canines**

***LEOPARD:* Sharp canine teeth, curved claws, jumping ability, agility**

The gorilla grabs the leopard's legs and yanks him off. The leopard's teeth leave a deep wound in the gorilla's neck. His sharp, curved claws rake into the gorilla's skin.

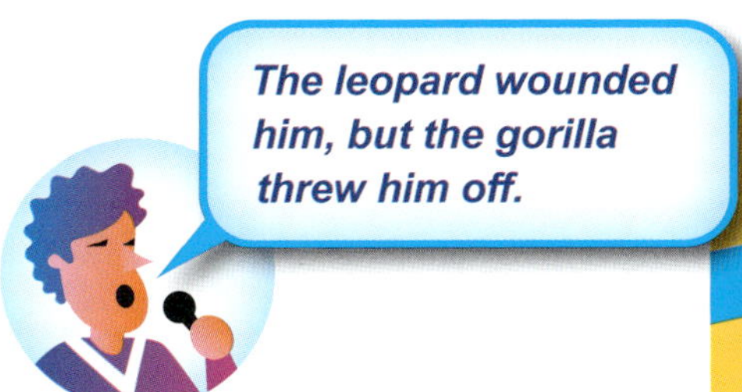

SCOREBOARD

	ROUND 8 SCORE	TOTAL SCORE
Gorilla	10	67
Leopard	8	73

FUN FACT
A leopard's shoulders are strong enough to carry a kill up to twice its weight high into a tree.

The gorilla tosses the leopard away. Like any cat, the leopard lands on his feet and springs at the gorilla again. The gorilla stands up to face his attacker. He wants to look big. But the cat's **agility** is outstanding. He leaps around the gorilla. The gorilla can't move as quickly. The leopard plans to pounce on his victim's back and bite the gorilla's neck.

The leopard jumps up and grabs the gorilla with his claws. His strong shoulders help him hang on, and his claws help him grip tightly. The leopard continues to bite the gorilla's neck. His claws grip tightly.

SCOREBOARD

	ROUND 9 SCORE	TOTAL SCORE
Gorilla	7	74
Leopard	10	83

DON'T CALL A GORILLA A MONKEY!

What's the difference between a gorilla and a monkey? A gorilla is a great ape. They don't have tails like monkeys. They also live longer and grow up more slowly. Gorillas are bigger and more intelligent. They can use tools and solve problems. They can even recognize themselves in a mirror.

The gorilla is still standing. He twists, trying to reach the leopard. The weight of the leopard pulls him off balance. He falls backward. The leopard's flexible body gets him mostly out from under the huge ape. But not completely. His front leg is injured as the gorilla lands on top of him. He's trapped.

The gorilla steps on the leopard. He bites him and pounds him with his fists. The leopard has had enough.

THINK ABOUT IT:
If the gorilla had been a blackback, would he still have won?

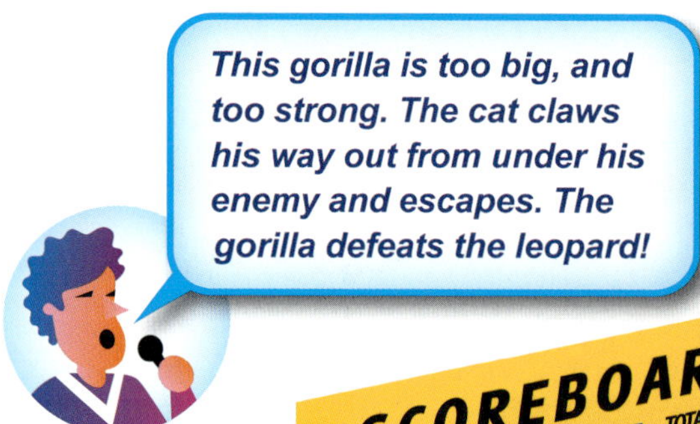

SCOREBOARD

	ROUND 10 SCORE	TOTAL SCORE
Gorilla	10	84
Leopard	0	83

BEYOND THE BOOK

After reading the book, it's time to think about what you learned. Try the following exercises to jump-start your ideas.

THINK

FIND OUT MORE. There is so much more to dig up about gorillas and leopards. What do you want to learn? Look them up on the web, or check out a book from the library. Maybe even visit them at the zoo!

CREATE

ART TIME. Which animal were you cheering for, the gorilla or the leopard? Now draw their picture. Look up a picture and grab some markers and paper. Will your gorilla or leopard be in its habitat? What will it be doing? Will it be with another animal? The sky is the limit!

SHARE

THE MORE WHO KNOW. Share what you learned about either gorillas or leopards. Use your own words to write a paragraph. What are the main ideas of this book? What facts from the book can you use to support those ideas? Share your paragraph with a classmate. Do they have any comments or questions?

GROW

HELP OUT! Many animals around the world are struggling to survive. Find an organization that is trying to save your favorite animal. Can you volunteer? Can your family donate to the organization's mission? You can also help by telling people about the animal. The more people who help, the safer the animal will be.

RESEARCH NINJA

Visit www.ninjaresearcher.com/5726 to learn how to take your research skills and book report writing to the next level!

DIGITAL LITERACY TOOLS

Research

SEARCH LIKE A PRO
Learn how to use search engines to find useful websites.

FACT OR FAKE
Discover how you can tell a trusted website from an untrustworthy resource.

TEXT DETECTIVE
Explore how to zero in on the information you need most.

SHOW YOUR WORK
Research responsibly–learn how to cite sources.

DOWNLOADABLE BOOK REPORT FORMS

Write

GET TO THE POINT
Learn how to express your main ideas.

PLAN OF ATTACK
Learn prewriting exercises and create an outline.

Further Resources

BOOKS

McManus, Lori. *Gorillas*. Chicago: Heinemann Library, 2012.

Mills, Andrea. *Big Cats*. New York: DK Publishing, 2019.

Patterson, Dr. Francine. *Koko's Kitten*. New York: Scholastic, 1985.

WEBSITES

FACTSURFER

Factsurfer.com gives you a safe, fun way to find more information.

1. Go to www.factsurfer.com.
2. Enter "Gorilla vs. Leopard" into the search box and click 🔍
3. Select your book cover to see a list of related websites.

Glossary

agility: The ability to move and change direction easily. The leopard's agility helps it hunt prey and move easily in difficult places.

ambush: To attack by surprise from a hidden place. A leopard will climb a tree to hide and then ambush its prey.

antelope: A fast-running, deer-like animal with horns and hooves. A leopard will chase an antelope at high speeds.

camouflage: Coloring that blends in with the location. A leopard's spots act as camouflage in the forest, behind rocks, or in tall grasses.

canine teeth: Pointy teeth next to the front teeth, also called fangs. A gorilla has large canine teeth.

carnivores: Animals that eat only meat. Leopards and other big cats are carnivores who hunt their prey.

herbivores: Animals that eat only plants. Gorillas are herbivores because they mostly eat plants.

intimidate: To cause another to feel afraid. A gorilla can intimidate other animals because of its large size.

opposable thumbs: Thumbs that can touch each of the other fingers. Gorillas have opposable thumbs, which help them grab things and pick them up like humans do.

prey: An animal that is being hunted by another animal for food. A leopard's favorite prey is an antelope.

Index

PHOTO CREDITS

The images in this book are reproduced through the courtesy of: Photography-by-Stretch/ Shutterstock Images, cover (top); Volodymyr Burdiak/Shutterstock Images, cover (bottom); Ammit Jack/Shutterstock Images, p. 3; pamas/Shutterstock Images, p. 4–5; Stu Porter/Shutterstock Images, p. 4–5; Denys.Kutsevalov/Shutterstock Images, p. 4–5; TravellingFatman/Shutterstock Images, p. 6; Dane Jorgensen/Shutterstock Images, p. 7; Yakov Oskanov/Shutterstock Images, p. 7; Roman Samokhin/Shutterstock Images, p. 8–9; BearFotos/Shutterstock Images, p. 8–9; Volodymyr Burdiak/Shutterstock Images, p. 9; Dane Jorgensen/Shutterstock Images, p. 9; meunierd/Shutterstock Images, p. 9; Nick Biemans/Shutterstock Images, p. 11; Lyle Gregg/ Shutterstock Images, p. 12; FCG/Shutterstock Images, p. 13; Kiki Dohmeier/Shutterstock Images, p. 14; dptro/Shutterstock Images, p. 16; Girish HC/Shutterstock Images, p. 17; Tanya Puntti/ Shutterstock Images, p. 18; Pavith Malaka/Shutterstock Images, p. 19; Anan Kaewkhammul/ Shutterstock Images, p. 20; Volodymyr Burdiak/Shutterstock Images, p. 21; Arunjunai/Shutterstock Images, p. 21; GUDKOV ANDREY/Shutterstock Images, p. 22; Joseph D Anthony/Shutterstock Images, p. 23; manfredstutz/Shutterstock Images, p. 24; Petr Salinger/Shutterstock Images, p. 25; Kerry Ring/Shutterstock Images, p. 25; CXI/Shutterstock Images, p. 26–27; Krakenimages.com/ Shutterstock Images, p. 30.

About the Author

Teresa Klepinger lives in the Pacific Northwest where she watches coyotes hunt, looks under rocks, and pokes things with sticks. She loves any kind of animal, storytelling, playing piano, reading lots of books, and most of all, her family.